MONTY

by James Stevenson

MULBERRY BOOKS • New York

FIRST PUBLISHED IN 1979 AND REISSUED IN 1992 BY GREENWILLOW BOOKS

A DIVISION OF WILLIAM MORROW & COMPANY, INC., 1350 AVENUE OF THE AMERICAS, NEW YORK, NY 10019. PRINTED IN HONG KONG BY SOUTH CHINA PRINTING COMPANY (1988) LTD.

FIRST MULBERRY EDITION, 1992. 10 9 8 7 6 5 4 3 2 1

WATERCOLOR PAINTS AND A BLACK PEN WERE USED FOR THE FULL-COLOR ART.

LIBRARY OF CONGRESS CATALOGING-IN-PUBLICATION DATA

STEVENSON, JAMES (DATE)
MONTY / BY JAMES STEVENSON.
P. CM.
SUMMARY: THE RABBIT, DUCK, AND FROG FIND THAT THEY HAVE NO WAY TO CROSS THE RIVER WHEN THEIR ALLIGATOR FRIEND, MONTY, TAKES A VACATION.
0-688-11288-9
[1. ALLIGATORS—FICTION. 2. ANIMALS—FICTION. 3. CARTOONS AND COMICS.] I. TITLE.
PZ7.S84748MON 1992
[E]—DC20 91-20657 CIP AC

To Jane Walker Stevenson

EVERY MORNING, ARTHUR AND DORIS AND TOM WALKED TO SCHOOL TOGETHER.

WHEN THEY CAME TO THE WIDE RIVER, THEY LOOKED FOR MONTY.

MONTY WAS ALWAYS ASLEEP, SNORING.
WAKE UP, MONTY! THIS IS A SCHOOL DAY!
GUG... GUGGLE.. GORGA...GUG...

HUH?
AGAIN?
YES. AND WE NEED A RIDE SO OUR BOOKS WON'T GET WET.
OOOOH.....
..O.K. ALL ABOARD!
YAWWWWN

THEY CLIMBED ON MONTY'S BACK, AND HE SWAM ACROSS THE RIVER.

WHEN THEY GOT TO THE FAR SIDE, DORIS AND ARTHUR AND TOM WENT TO SCHOOL. MONTY WENT BACK TO SLEEP.

EVERY AFTERNOON, HE GAVE THEM A RIDE BACK.
HURRY UP! WE WANT TO GET HOME!
MORE TO THE RIGHT!
DON'T GET OUR BOOKS WET!

...BUT MONTY DID NOT COME.

THEN MONTY FLOATED BY.
MONTY! WHERE HAVE YOU BEEN?
I AM ON VACATION.
THIS IS NOT VACATION TIME!
IT IS FOR ME. THIS IS ALLIGATOR VACATION.

ALLIGATOR VACATION ??
WHAT'S THAT ?
IT'S WHEN NOBODY TELLS ALLIGATORS WHAT TO DO.
HOW LONG DOES IT LAST ?
YEARS AND YEARS, SOMETIMES
...THEN MONTY WAS GONE.

WELL, WHAT ARE WE SUPPOSED TO DO NOW?
IT BEATS ME.
EVERYBODY START THINKING.

WHAT ARE YOU THINKING, DORIS?
I'M THINKING WE NEED A NEW ALLIGATOR.
THAT'S NOT THINKING. THAT'S JUST WISHING.

WELL, I CAN'T THINK WITH ALL THIS THINKING GOING ON AROUND ME...
THEN GO THINK SOMEPLACE ELSE.
THAT'S JUST WHAT I'LL DO.

NICE AND QUIET HERE..
..A PERFECT PLACE TO THINK.
HI, DORIS! HI, DORIS!
WHAT ARE YOU DOING?
I'M THINKING.
WOW-LET'S WATCH!
LOOK AT HER THINKING!
THINK, THINK, THINK---
QUIET!

PARDON US FOR LIVING...
WHO WANTS TO WATCH A DUCK THINK, ANYWAY?

THAT'S ALL I NEED--FOUR TURTLES...
...ALL I NEED?
HEY, TURTLES! WAIT!

ARTHUR AND TOM
WERE STILL THINKING, WHEN...
I GOT IT!

WHAT DO WE DO, DORIS ?
FIRST YOU STEP ON TURTLE NUMBER ONE, THEN YOU STEP ON TURTLE NUMBER TWO, THEN THREE AND FOUR--- AND YOU'RE ACROSS !

TURTLE NUMBER FOUR---
WHERE ARE YOU?

SPLASH

ARE YOU LOOKING FOR ME?
NOT ANY MORE.

THEY WENT BACK TO SHORE, AND PUT THEIR BOOKS IN THE SUN TO DRY. TOM AND DORIS SAT DOWN.

HEY...I FOUND A BOARD!

IT'S TOO LITTLE TO FLOAT ON.
TOO SHORT FOR A BRIDGE.
I KNOW. I HAVE A BETTER IDEA.

HERE'S MY PLAN: YOU SIT ON THE BOARD, TOM.. AND I'LL JUMP OUT OF THE TREE ONTO THE OTHER END OF THE BOARD, AND YOU'LL GO FLYING RIGHT ACROSS THE RIVER!

OH, BOY!

THEY DECIDED TO TRY IT WITH DORIS BECAUSE SHE WAS THE LIGHTEST. DORIS STOOD ON THE BOARD.

BETTER,
BUT NOT PERFECT.
SPLASH

IT WAS CLEAR THAT THEY WOULD HAVE TO SWIM ACROSS.
HANG ON, TOM..
KEEP THE BOOKS DRY
STEADY.. HERE WE GO..
MORE TO THE RIGHT, ARTHUR
SLOW DOWN
GO FASTER
STRAIGHT AHEAD, ARTHUR
DON'T WOBBLE ARTHUR
SIT STILL TOM
BE QUIET
STOP TELLING ME WHAT TO DO!
STOP TELLING ME WHAT TO DO!
STOP TELLING ME WHAT TO DO!

HOW CAN MONTY STAND THIS?
AND TWICE A DAY.
POOR MONTY.
HEY, I'M SLIPPING!
WE NEED MONTY!
I'M SINKING!
--AND QUICK.

SUDDENLY, THEY FELT SOMETHING UNDER THEM.
..HEY, IT'S MONTY!
THANKS, MONTY!
SAVED!
HOORAY!
YOU'RE A PAL, MONTY!
NO PROBLEM!
NOTICE HOW MONTY GOES JUST THE RIGHT SPEED?
AND HE STEERS PERFECTLY, TOO!
I LOVE THE WAY MONTY SWIMS.

WE THOUGHT YOU WERE ON VACATION...
I AM, BUT SOMETIMES WHEN I AM ON VACATION I TAKE A DAY OFF

THANKS FOR THE RIDE, MONTY!
IS THERE ANY CHANCE YOU'LL BE HERE THIS AFTERNOON, MONTY?
MONTY?
GUG... GUGGLE...
BUT MONTY HAD ALREADY STARTED TO SNORE.